FLUFFY
GOES TO SCHOOL

*Dedicated to Sharon Zwick
and her first grade class at
Bedford Village Elementary School*

*To Maxwell Crook
— K.M.*

*To Matthew
— M.S.*

Text copyright © 1997 by Kate McMullan.
Illustrations copyright © 1997 Mavis Smith.

All rights reserved. Published by Scholastic Inc.
SCHOLASTIC, CARTWHEEL BOOKS, FLUFFY THE CLASSROOM GUINEA PIG,
and associated logos are trademarks and/or registered trademarks of Scholastic Inc.
Lexile is a registered trademark of MetaMetrics, Inc.

Library of Congress Cataloging-in-Publication Data is available.

ISBN-13: 978-0-590-37213-8
ISBN-10: 0-590-37213-0

15 14 13 12 11   09 10 11 12/0

Printed in the U.S.A. 23 • This edition first printing, July 2008

FLUFFY
GOES TO SCHOOL

GROWING READER
LEVEL 3
700-1500 WORDS

by Kate McMullan
Illustrated by Mavis Smith

Cartwheel
·B·O·O·K·S·®

SCHOLASTIC INC.
New York Toronto London Auckland Sydney
Mexico City New Delhi Hong Kong Buenos Aires

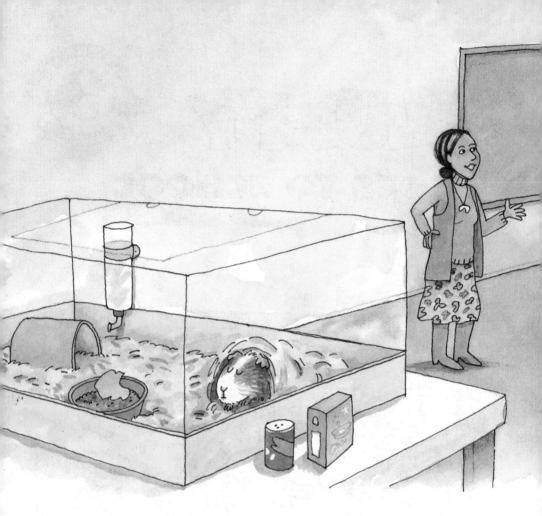

Hello, Fluffy!

"Close your eyes," said Ms. Day.
"We will pick a name for our new guinea pig."
The guinea pig had his eyes closed.
He was sleeping under some straw.

"How many want Sparky?" asked Ms. Day.

Emma raised her hand.

"How many want Ringo?" asked Ms. Day.

Maxwell raised his hand.

"How many want Fluffy?" asked Ms. Day.

Everybody else raised a hand.

"Open your eyes," said Ms. Day.
"Our guinea pig's name is Fluffy."

"All right!" said Jasmine.
She and Wade slapped hands.

Maxwell walked over
to the guinea pig cage.
"Hello, Fluffy," he said.
The guinea pig opened his eyes.
Fluffy? he thought. **Who is Fluffy?**
Had another animal come into his cage?

The guinea pig looked in his tunnel.

Come out, Fluffy! he growled.

Or I will pull you out!

But no animal came out.

The guinea pig ran over to his food dish.
Get away from my food, Fluffy! he said.
Back away and no one gets hurt.
But no animal was in the food dish.

Two hands picked up the guinea pig.
"Hello, Fluffy!" said Ms. Day.
Fluffy? thought the guinea pig.
Me? You must be joking!

"Hello, Fluffy!" said the whole class.

Fluffy is not a good name for me!

thought the guinea pig. **I'm big and strong!**

"Fluffy is sweet!" said Jasmine.

No way! thought the guinea pig.

I am one bad pig!

"He's so cute!" said Emma.

The hands put Fluffy back in the cage.

I'm out of here, thought the guinea pig.

He went under the straw again.

Soon he was sleeping.

He dreamed that his name was Butch.

Fluffy to the Rescue

Emma and Wade made Fluffy a play yard.
Wade put in a box, a coconut shell,
and a cardboard tube.
Emma put in Fluffy.

Fluffy jumped into the box.
He pretended it was a police car
and he was a policeman.
He chased some robbers.
Stop! called Officer Fluffy.
And I mean now!

"Why are you making so much noise?"
asked Wade.
You are under arrest,
thought Officer Fluffy.

Wade put Fluffy in the coconut shell.

Fluffy pretended it was a boat.

The boat rocked in the storm.

Captain Fluffy held the wheel steady.

The passengers were afraid.

Don't worry, Captain Fluffy told them.
I will save you.

"Stop rocking," Emma said.

"You will get sick."

I never get seasick, thought Captain Fluffy.

Emma picked Fluffy up.

She put him down by the tube.

It looked like a spaceship to Fluffy.

Help! Commander Fluffy!

cried one of the crew.

Space rocks are about to hit the ship!

Commander Fluffy sat down.
Put on your seat belts, he said.
This will be a bumpy ride!
Commander Fluffy turned the spaceship
away from a big space rock.

Commander Fluffy turned the spaceship
away from another space rock.
He did it again and again.
Hooray for Commander Fluffy!
shouted the crew.

Now the ship flew into deep space.

But what was this?

Another ship was racing toward them!

Out of the ship came a giant hand!

It turned Commander Fluffy's spaceship

upside down.

Take the ship, crew!

Commander Fluffy called.

I will save you from the giant hand!

"Come out of that tube," said Emma.

Take me to your leader,

thought Commander Fluffy.

Emma put Fluffy back in his cage.
"Have a carrot," said Wade.
Fluffy went to his food dish.
A carrot is good, he thought,
after a hard day at work.

Fluffy the Fast Thinker

Emma took her doll over to Fluffy's cage.

"Fluffy," said Emma, "this is Baby."

Hi, Baby, thought Fluffy.

"Fluffy, would you like to try on Baby's dress?" asked Jasmine.

No way, thought Fluffy. **Not me!**

Jasmine and Emma put Baby's dress
on Fluffy.
"So pretty!" said Jasmine.
Get me out of here! thought Fluffy.

"Would you like to try on Baby's hat?"
said Jasmine.
No! No! No! No! thought Fluffy.
Emma put Baby's hat on Fluffy's head.
Jasmine tied it under his chin.
"What a little doll!" said Emma.

"Look at baby Fluffy, Ms. Day," said Emma.

"Very cute," said Ms. Day. "But do you think Fluffy is happy dressed up like that?"

"Sure he is," said Emma.

"He loves it," said Jasmine.

Wrong! thought Fluffy.

Wrong! Wrong! Wrong!

"May we show baby Fluffy
to Ms. Zwick?" asked Emma.
"She was our teacher last year."
"All right," said Ms. Day.
"Just be careful with him."

Jasmine carefully carried Fluffy into
Ms. Zwick's room.
But no one was there.
"Look," said Emma.
"Ms. Zwick's class has a guinea pig, too!"

The girls walked over to see it.
A sign on its cage said DUKE.
"Duke!" Emma called. "Meet Fluffy!"
This can't be happening, thought
Fluffy.

Jasmine put Fluffy down
by Duke's cage.
Duke opened his eyes
and looked at Fluffy.
Who are you?
asked Duke.
WHAT are you?

Fluffy thought fast.

I am a spy, he said.

I am on a secret mission.

That is why I have on these silly clothes.

Wow, said Duke.

"It's time to go, Fluffy," Jasmine said.

"Say good-bye to your new friend."

Duty calls, Fluffy told Duke.

Wow, Duke said again.

Don't tell anyone that you saw me here,
said Fluffy.

I won't say a word, sir, said Duke.

Emma and Jasmine carried Fluffy back to their classroom. They took off the doll clothes and put Fluffy back in his cage. **That was a close one,** thought Fluffy.